# Jeanie & Genie

## LARGER THAN LIFE

★★ BY **TRISH GRANTED**

ILLUSTRATED BY **MANUELA LÓPEZ**

**LITTLE SIMON**

New York  London  Toronto  Sydney  New Delhi

 **LITTLE SIMON**

An imprint of Simon & Schuster Children's Publishing Division
1230 Avenue of the Americas, New York, New York 10020
First Little Simon paperback edition June 2023
Copyright © 2023 by Simon & Schuster, Inc.
All rights reserved, including the right of reproduction in whole or in part in any form.
LITTLE SIMON is a registered trademark of Simon & Schuster, Inc., and associated colophon is a trademark of Simon & Schuster, Inc.
For information about special discounts for bulk purchases, please contact Simon & Schuster Special Sales at 1-866-506-1949 or business@simonandschuster.com.
The Simon & Schuster Speakers Bureau can bring authors to your live event. For more information or to book an event contact the Simon & Schuster Speakers Bureau at 1-866-248-3049 or visit our website at www.simonspeakers.com.
Designed by Brittany Fetcho
Manufactured in the United States of America 0423 LAK
10 9 8 7 6 5 4 3 2 1
This book has been cataloged with the Library of Congress.
ISBN 978-1-6659-3588-3 (hc)
ISBN 978-1-6659-3587-6 (pbk)
ISBN 978-1-6659-3589-0 (ebook)

# TABLE OF CONTENTS

# DINO-MITE!

Jeanie Bell started every weekday the same: She brushed her teeth, got dressed, checked her homework twice, and quietly ate a bowl of cereal while she thought about the day ahead.

But not today. Today her little brother Jake came crashing down the stairs just as Jeanie was pouring the milk in her bowl.

"It's here! It's here!" screamed Jake.

Jeanie was so startled she dropped the milk, and it splattered across the table.

"Jake!" she yelled as she grabbed some napkins to sop up the spill.

Jeanie's mom folded her newspaper and took off her reading glasses. "What's here?" she asked Jake.

"The Dinosaur Safari exhibit at the zoo!" Jake cried. "I've been waiting foreeeeeever for it to open. And it's finally going to. This weekend!" Jake raced around the breakfast table, flapping his arms and roaring. "I'm going to fly like a pterodactyl!"

"If you don't slow down, I'm going to be *pterrifyingly* sick." Jeanie rolled her eyes as she finished cleaning up the mess. "Anyway, what's so special about some exhibit at the zoo?"

Jake stuck out his tongue. "It's not 'some exhibit.' It's a safari. Of *dinosaurs*. They have these life-size dino-robots that really roar!"

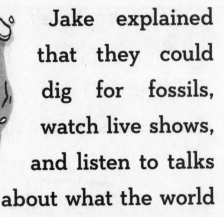

Jake explained that they could dig for fossils, watch live shows, and listen to talks about what the world was like when some of the biggest creatures in history roamed the earth. Plus they could get their picture taken with a T. rex! Even Jeanie had to admit that sounded pretty cool.

"Okay, Jakey, we'll go this weekend." Mrs. Bell tapped her newspaper. "Besides, the *Rivertown Gazette* says the botanical garden next door is getting in on the act. They're going to have a display of dinosaur topiaries that I'd love to see," she said. She turned to Jeanie. "Want to invite Willow? You girls can have a sleepover here afterward."

Jeanie brightened at that idea. She loved the gardens. And she knew Willow had never been—Willow had only moved to Rivertown recently. Jeanie really hoped her friend would want to come, otherwise she'd be in for a *long* weekend following Jake around!

But Jeanie had to wait all morning to invite Willow. At school, Ms. Patel gave classroom 2B a quiz. Then their art teacher, Mr. Bloom, taught them a drawing lesson on perspective.

"Sometimes the best ideas come when you look at the world from a new angle," he said while the class sketched a sunflower in a vase.

Jeanie tried to put the safari out of her mind and concentrate on her drawing. But it just looked like a flower.

She glanced at Willow's sketch, which showed a bright yellow blossom shining down on Rivertown from the sky.

"See it's a *sun* flower!" Willow explained.

Jeanie smiled to herself. That was very imaginative . . . and *very* Willow.

Willow wasn't like any friend Jeanie had ever had before. She was funny and creative and downright magical. Like, *literally* magical. Because Willow was a genie! Well, a genie-in-training. She was still learning to control her powers while training to be a Master Genie. For now, whenever someone looked her in the eyes and said the words "I wish," Willow *had* to grant their heart's desire, whether she wanted to or not. And that made for some exciting—and complicated—moments.

By the time recess came around,

13

Jeanie was practically bursting to ask Willow if she wanted to come on the family zoo outing.

"A dinosaur safari exhibit?!"

Willow's eyes lit up, just as Jeanie had hoped they would. "*Dino*-mite! Count me in!"

# Chapter 2

# GOING WILD

Willow Davis woke up early on Saturday morning. She'd never been to a zoo before, but she loved animals. *I can't wait to get wild*, she thought, laughing at her own joke. Though hopefully things wouldn't be as wild as the time she'd accidentally conjured up penguins at the ice rink!

As she got dressed, Willow made one very big wish. *Please don't let me grant any wishes today, she thought. The zoo is enough of an adventure without any magic!*

Willow quickly put on a leopard-print T-shirt, tiger-striped skirt, and zebra-print leggings. She checked to make sure her magic lamp charm necklace was secure around her neck, and now she was ready to rock and roll!

Downstairs, Mrs. Davis was making pancakes for breakfast—Willow's favorite!

"I thought we were out of syrup!" Willow exclaimed as she sat down at the table.

Willow's mom gave her a wink.

*Oh right!* Willow thought. When you were a genie, you never *had* to go to the store. And Willow's mom wasn't just any genie. She was the president of the World Genie Association, and the most magical person Willow knew! Willow wasn't sure she'd ever be as good at granting wishes as her mom was, but she sure would try.

And yet somehow, without any spells at all, Willow made her pancakes disappear!

"What kind of car does an elephant drive?" she joked as she led her mom to the driveway. "One with a big trunk!"

Willow's mom laughed and hopped into the car. Soon they were on their way to the Bells' house.

"I bet Jake is really excited," said Mrs. Davis.

Willow nodded in agreement. Jake got excited about, well, everything—but especially dinosaurs. He'd probably been roaring like a velociraptor for hours. And if Willow knew her best friend, Jeanie had probably been *annoyed* for hours.

Willow just hoped Jeanie wouldn't wish for Jake to disappear again. That had been one of the craziest wishes Willow had ever granted . . . and the hardest to reverse!

When they arrived, Willow waved goodbye to her mom and ran into the Bells' house without knocking. She couldn't wait to find Jeanie and get going on their animal adventure!

"Wow!" Jeanie said when Willow found her in the kitchen. "That's some outfit!"

"Don't you love it?" Willow gushed. "I thought this would help me blend in at the zoo."

Jeanie grinned. "It's . . ."

"Awesome!" cried Jake. He tore through the kitchen, a winged-dinosaur cape flying behind him. "Now let's go, go, GO!"

Willow giggled. She had a feeling she was in for a *roaring* good time.

# Chapter 3

# THE ALMOST-WISH

By the time they got their tickets and headed inside, Jeanie had forgotten to be annoyed with Jake. She remembered all the things she liked about the zoo.

The bird pavilion fluttered with bursts of brilliant colors. The sea lions showed off their moves. And the café sold delicious lemonade that came in giraffe-shaped cups.

"Okay, kids. There are info booths all along this main path," said Mrs. Bell. "If we get separated, find one and tell an adult."

"Enough talking," cried Jake. "It's time to see some dinosaurs!"

"We'll get there," said Mr. Bell. "But the Dinosaur Safari exhibit is at the other end of the zoo. So let's visit some of the other animals along the way, huh, kiddo?"

Jake huffed.

"It's not like the animatronic dinosaurs are *going* anywhere," Jeanie pointed out to her brother. "They'll still be there in an hour."

The family wandered over to the elephant enclosure, where a trio of elephants were walking around. The littlest one dipped its trunk in some water and sprayed it all over its mother.

"They're so playful!" Jeanie said
to Willow. "And they seem like such
sweet creatures."

But Willow wasn't listening. She
was whispering something under
her breath.

"Are you . . . talking to them?"
Jeanie asked her.

Willow blushed. "It wouldn't be the first time I spoke to an animal and it understood me."

Jeanie giggled as they kept going down the path. They were heading toward the lions.

Up ahead, a little girl stood in front of the glass partition. She was staring longingly at a fuzzy lion cub. When she put her hand up, the cub raised its paw.

The little girl turned to her father. "Daddy, I wish—"

Jeanie's eyes went wide. She grabbed Willow's arm and dragged her away from the exhibit as fast as she could.

"Hey! What was that all about?" Willow asked when they stopped in front of the alligator pond.

"That girl," Jeanie said breathlessly. "She was going to make a wish. And there is *no* way that can happen today. *Especially* not near the lions."

"Ohh," said Willow, understanding. "You're right."

"Maybe we should try to stay away from the dangerous animals altogether," Jeanie suggested. She glanced at the alligators, whose pointy white teeth glistened brightly in the sunlight.

"That's sounds like a good idea," said Willow. "Do you know what alligators call slowpokes?"

Jeanie shook her head.

"Dinner." Willow shivered. "Let's get out of here!"

# Chapter 4

# IT'S A T. REX! IT'S ALIVE!

An hour later, Willow was grinning from ear to ear. She'd seen a family of otters, a sleepy-looking koala, and some roly-poly pandas snacking on bamboo.

And now she and the Bells had finally reached the Dinosaur Safari exhibit! Jake zigzagged from one animatronic dinosaur to the next, spouting every fact he knew about the creatures. He ran past the stage. It was empty right now, but Willow bet that someday Jake would be giving the expert talk there.

"Doesn't that iguanodon look like Zora Klein's pet lizard?" she whispered to Jeanie as they continued down the path.

"It does!" Jeanie agreed.

Willow looked around. She understood why Jake had been so excited. These dinosaurs were so lifelike—and they all moved in different ways! Some flapped their wings; some opened their mouths; some moved their arms.

"I'm hungry," said Jeanie. "Want to go grab some popcorn?" She pointed at the Snackasauraus Hut.

Willow shook her head. Jake had found the massive T. rex and was already posing for pictures with it. "No, I'm going to get a picture of me and Mr. Rex over there for my mom!"

So Jeanie headed off to the snack bar while Willow caught up with Jake.

They took a few silly shots pretending to be scared of the giant dino. Well, sort of pretending. When the T. rex roared, Willow briefly forgot it was a robot, and she jumped back in surprise! She was so shaken that she almost didn't hear Jake.

"I wish these dinosaurs were real," he whispered, glancing at Willow.

The back of Willow's neck began to tingle. Then her lamp charm began to glow with a warm golden light.

Willow's heart skipped a beat. She knew what that meant.

So did Jeanie, who was back with a big tub of popcorn. "Willow!" she cried, pointing at the necklace. "Whatever that wish was...don't grant it!"

"I can't help it!" Willow watched in horror as her charm's golden rays of magic circled the animatronic dinosaurs.

The T. rex cocked its head, looked down at Willow, and then stepped onto the path.

It was . . . alive!

The T. rex blinked twice, then ran toward the exit faster than Willow had ever seen anything move.

And it wasn't alone. Soon all the dinosaurs were coming to life and leaving the safety of the exhibit!

"What are we going to do?" Jeanie said, panicked.

Willow looked around and suddenly had an idea. She ran over to the empty stage and grabbed the microphone.

"Hello, everyone!" Her voice boomed through the speakers. All the visitors turned to stare. "Um . . . welcome to the *theatrical* portion of the exhibit! At the Rivertown Zoo, we bring science to life!"

For a long moment, no one said anything. But when a triceratops head-butted the SAFARI sign, the whole crowd burst into applause.

"Um . . . yes . . . that was all part of the exhibit!" Willow cried. "Enjoy the show!"

Willow stepped away from the microphone. She needed to reverse Jake's wish . . . and fast.

Otherwise her first visit to the zoo might be her last!

# Chapter 5

# DINOS ON THE LOOSE

Jeanie was impressed. Willow's quick thinking had everyone at the zoo convinced that the dinosaurs were acting exactly as they were supposed to.

But she knew that this was a temporary fix. She and her best friend still had a dino-size problem on their hands.

"Can you believe this?!" Jake

cried. "This safari is even better than I imagined. We have to follow the dinosaurs and see how the show ends!"

"No!" cried Willow. "I mean . . . um . . . Jeanie, what do I mean?"

Jeanie looked around the exhibit frantically. "Jake, you *can't* leave before visiting the gift shop. I think I see a build-your-own-dinosaur display. Don't you want a souvenir from the best day ever?"

Jake's eyes lit up. "Can I, Mom? Pretty please?"

Mrs. Bell chuckled. "What a thoughtful suggestion, Jeanie," she said. "Okay, Jakey, but only one toy."

Jeanie thought fast. "Dad, while you guys are helping Jake, can Willow and I go see the sloths? Her mom loves them, and we promised we'd take a picture for her."

"Sure, honey," said Mr. Bell. "Jake will probably be as slow as those sloths, so take your time."

Jeanie thanked her dad, caught Willow's eye, and ran for it.

At the big fountain in the zoo's main plaza, the girls stopped and looked around. There were raptors playing catch with a ball, two spiny-looking dinosaurs at the butterfly carousel, and a small plesiosaur in the fountain.

Jeanie looked around. "Willow, *how* do we fix this?" she asked her friend.

Before Willow could answer, a shout came from the playground. "Woo-hoo! This is the coolest!"

A group of little kids was climbing a stegosaurus like a rock wall as their parents calmly stood by and watched. Every so often the stegosaurus would take a step, shaking the kids and making them giggle.

"The zoo has really gone all out this year," said one of the dads. "The display is so much better than last year's."

Just then a pterodactyl swooped down and snatched the hat right off his head.

The man's jaw dropped. "How did they do that?"

Willow turned back to Jeanie. "At least no one's noticed the dinos are *real*."

"That's true," said Jeanie.

But as she watched a long-necked dinosaur sneak up to a picnic table and steal a hot dog straight out of someone's hands, she knew it wouldn't last.

Eventually someone would realize that animatronic dinosaurs couldn't really fly. Or eat.

And then she and Willow would have some explaining to do. . . .

# ONE . . . TWO . . . JUMP!

On the outside, Willow was making jokes and trying to remain calm. But on the inside, she was panicking. If she couldn't reverse the wish, she'd never prove to the WGA that she was ready to become a Master Genie. Plus, who knew what would happen with all these dinosaurs on the loose!

*Ugh.* If only she was as good at wish granting as she was at drawing silly pictures. She could really use one of Mr. Bloom's inspirational pep talks right about now. . . .

"Wait a second. That's it!" Willow cried.

"What's it?" asked Jeanie.

"I think I know how to figure this out," Willow said. "Come on!"

She led Jeanie to the Treetop Escape—a giant play area that had rope bridges, zip lines, and wooden forts built high in the trees.

Jeanie looked wary. "Um, Willow, what are we going to do up there?" she asked as a brontosaurus chomped leaves from the treetops above, sprinkling the girls with falling bits of foliage.

But Willow couldn't tell Jeanie the plan. Her friend would never agree to something so . . . risky. And Willow didn't have any other ideas.

"Just trust me," she said confidently.

But as they climbed a very wobbly rope ladder, Willow's confidence began to slip. She was only a genie-in-training, and her plan would require some serious magic.

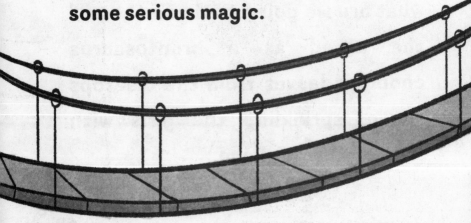

So she tried to focus on the advice their art teacher had given them earlier that week. And by the time she reached the platform at the top of the ladder, she was sure she was onto a good idea.

"Okay," Jeanie huffed as Willow helped her to her feet. "*What* is going on?"

"Remember what Mr. Bloom said? About how the best ideas come when you look at the world from a new angle? Well, I thought if we could get a better view of all the action down there"—she pointed to the chaotic scene below—"then maybe I'd know how to reverse the wish."

"So we came up here for the view?" Jeanie looked doubtful.

"Nope," Willow replied. "We're going up *there* for the view." She pointed at the brontosaurus, who was still happily munching away on his lunch. "On the count of three, we're jumping onto that dinosaur."

"Oh no we're not," said Jeanie. "That's . . . that's . . . ridiculous. Dangerous. AGAINST THE RULES!"

"There are no rules for how to deal with dinosaurs," said Willow. "And anyway, do you have a better idea?"

Jeanie sighed. She did not.

"Okay, then." Willow grabbed Jeanie's hand. "On the count of three. One . . . two . . ."

And then Willow jumped.

# A WILD RIDE

"AHHHH!" Jeanie screamed.

*Thump!* The girls landed hard on the brontosaurus's back.

Jeanie scrambled to grab hold of the dinosaur's neck as it finished its lunch.

"I can't believe we're doing this!" she cried.

But as Jeanie looked around, she had to admit that Willow was right—they did have a pretty good view from up here.

"Look!" Willow pointed to the playground. Jeanie saw that the stegosaurus was running in circles, the little kids flying from its spikes like flags waving in the breeze.

Suddenly a bunch of raptors ran

by. The stegosaurus stopped circling, shook the kids off onto a soft patch of grass, and sprinted after the pack of wild beasts.

"Where are they all going?" Willow wanted to know.

"I don't know," said Jeanie. "But I think we're going to find out. . . ."

The brontosaurus snorted and took off after the stampede. Jeanie and Willow hung on for dear life as the dinosaur raced through the zoo.

They flew past the meerkat prairie, where tons of furry heads popped up to watch them. The birds in the aviary all squawked, and the screeches coming from the monkey house were loud enough for Jeanie to cover her ears. Except she couldn't. Because she had to hold on to the brontosaurus.

"We're leaving the zoo!" Willow cried when they zoomed through the entrance gate a few minutes later.

"Yeah," Jeanie yelled back. But as she glanced around, she realized all the dinosaurs were taking a familiar path. "And I think I know where we're headed."

The brontosaurus slowed to a trot as they approached the botanical garden. For a long moment, Jeanie forgot to be afraid. The garden was as pretty as ever. But where there were usually only rosebushes and cherry blossoms, the garden was now filled with huge topiary sculptures . . . in the shape of their new prehistoric pals.

"The gardeners here are so talented," Jeanie gushed. Then she shook her head. She couldn't get distracted when there was still a wish gone wild to tame!

Their brontosaurus ambled around the garden, munching on apple trees and peonies until it came to a stop in front of a small topiary with a long graceful neck.

"It found another brontosaurus!" said Willow.

Jeanie giggled as the dinosaur nuzzled the little green sculpture. "Aww, and it thinks this one is its baby!"

As the brontosaurus rubbed its head against the topiary's neck, a gardener in overalls caught Jeanie's eye. The woman's jaw dropped, and she looked like she might be reaching for her phone.

Jeanie couldn't let the secret of her friend's magic get out. Not if Willow wanted to become a Master Genie someday.

"Um, Willow?" Jeanie whispered. "We need to reverse this wish. *Now!*"

# Chapter 8

# THE FLY-AWAY SPELL

Willow's mind raced. She tried to remember every charm and spell she'd ever learned. Surely one of them would help fix this wish!

She'd earned the Reverse the Curse badge for figuring out how to make Jake return when Jeanie had wished him away.

She'd gotten the Basic Gifting badge for all the times she'd conjured up a pizza on sleepover nights.

And she'd earned the Making Unwanted Things Disappear badge for helping her mom deal with a pesky lunar eclipse that had made the whole town go haywire.

That had been one of the hardest. Even though Willow had practiced all the disappearing magic in her mother's library, she'd still had some trouble remembering the fly-away spell. But with help from her best friend—and best study partner ever—Willow had made everything float back to where it belonged.

*That's it!* thought Willow.

"I think I know what to do," she told Jeanie. "But first we need to get off this brontosaurus!"

"Can you get us closer to that huge diplodocus topiary?" Jeanie asked.

"I think so," said Willow. She considered using magic, but right now she *really* didn't want to tempt fate. So instead, she put one last wild plan into motion.

She'd noticed that a pteranodon had been circling the area for a little while. She put two fingers in her mouth and whistled as loud as she could, and the flying dinosaur swooped right over! Jeanie gave Willow a surprised look, but Willow just shrugged. She had communicated with animals before—why not dinosaurs? "Hop on!" she told Jeanie.

The two girls climbed onto the pteranodon, and Willow leaned forward, hoping the dinosaur would know to fly downward. Somehow it worked! The dinosaur gently coasted to the ground, and Willow and Jeanie climbed off.

And now it was time for Willow to *really* work her magic. She pulled Jeanie behind a rosebush so they wouldn't be seen.

Then she began to chant. "Dinos, dinos, all of you, fly away back to the zoo! Dinos, dinos, all of you, fly away back to the zoo!"

Suddenly her golden lamp charm began to glow. A light breeze rustled through the trees, picking up speed until it was a full-blown gust of wind. It whistled through the topiary sculptures, rattling the branches and blowing some leaves right off.

"Brrr!" said Jeanie as the wind got stronger. It whirled and swirled around all the dinosaurs, lifting each one high into the air . . . up, up, up, until they were all out of sight.

"I know I've done that fly-away spell before," whispered Willow. "But I never get used to seeing it in action!"

As the wind finally died down, she and Jeanie crept out from their hiding spot.

"Willow, you did it!" cried Jeanie.

Willow nodded. She'd made the dinosaurs disappear, but had she returned them to their proper place at the zoo? There was only one way to find out.

# Chapter 9

# SUPER-MEGA DISTRACTIONS

"It's not much farther!" Willow huffed and puffed.

Jeanie *definitely* wasn't a runner. Gym was the only subject at school she didn't like.

But right now she was running back to the Dinosaur Safari exhibit as fast as her legs would carry her. She and Willow had to find out if the spell had worked!

101

As far as Jeanie could tell, the zoo seemed totally normal. Magic free.

And when they finally got back to the Dinosaur Safari, to both Jeanie's and Willow's amazement, all the dinosaurs were exactly where they belonged.

"It worked!" Jeanie squealed. She gave Willow a high five. "See, studying and practicing really *do* pay off!"

Willow smiled. "I couldn't have done it without you!"

"Hey, you two!" called Jeanie's mom. "You're back! And just in time to see the totally awesome super-mega dinosaur Jake built at the gift shop."

"Where did you guys go, anyway?" asked Jake. "I forgot to tell you I saw a sign that said the sloth habitat was closed today and—"

"What makes your dinosaur so super-mega awesome?" Jeanie interrupted.

"Yeah, Jake," said Willow. "Can it fly or swim or run?"

Jake's face lit up. "It can fly *and* swim *and* run . . . really fast."

"Hopefully not as fast as some of the dinosaurs we saw today!" Jeanie's dad chuckled. "The animatronics were so realistic this year!"

Jeanie's mom nodded. "The zoo must have spent a fortune on them!"

"Yup," said Jeanie. "It was a really . . . wild . . . exhibit."

"What I want to know is how they got that robotic triceratops to knock over the fence with its horns," said Jake. "That seems like something only a *real* dinosaur could do. . . ."

Jeanie and Willow looked at each other for a second, then burst into laughter.

"Don't be ridiculous," Jeanie said to Jake.

"Hey, Jake," said Willow. "What do you call dinosaur twins?"

Jake thought for a moment.

"A pair-o-dactyls!" Willow said. Now Jake was laughing too. And good thing, because it was *almost* as if he was onto them.

On the ride home, Willow kept everyone distracted with more jokes, and Jeanie thought about what they would do at their sleepover that night. One thing was certain: There would be *no* wishes. Although she sure was in the mood for pizza. Okay, maybe there was room for one more wish.

# Chapter 10

# ONE STEP CLOSER

The next morning Willow could barely keep her eyes open at the Bells' breakfast table.

She and Jeanie had stayed up reliving their lucky escape at the zoo, sneaking downstairs for chocolate chip cookies, and telling stories by flashlight late into the night.

But feeling a little sleepy was worth it. She'd had a great weekend hanging with her best friend. And now she was having the perfect breakfast. Pancakes again!

"Can you please pass the syrup?" she asked after a big yawn.

"Sure, sleepyhead," teased Jeanie as Mr. Bell flipped on the television. The channel 7 weather report was just beginning.

"I'm here at the Rivertown Botanical Garden," meteorologist Storm Hunter said. "Yesterday, a surprise windstorm left a trail of chaos—and piles and piles of leaves. Here to tell us about it is head gardener Rosie Choi."

He angled his microphone toward a small woman wearing a very big hat who looked completely baffled.

"It was the funniest thing," said Rosie. "The breeze picked up so fast, we didn't have a chance to secure the topiary dinosaurs we had on display."

"Now they look a bit more like dinosaur skeletons," Willow whispered in between bites of pancake.

Jeanie giggled.

"That's not what dinosaur skeletons look like," said Jake. "The average dinosaur has over two hundred bones, not some skinny little branches."

"Well, at least it's a lot calmer today!" said Mr. Bell. "Girls, if you're all done, you can put your plates in the sink and go outside. I'll handle cleanup."

"Thanks, Mr. Bell!" said Willow. Then she and Jeanie headed out. Willow spotted a small rectangle of fresh dirt.

"What's that for?" she asked.

"My mom and I are going to plant a garden," said Jeanie.

Willow pretended to think. "With dinosaur-shaped topiaries?" she asked slyly.

"Um, no," said Jeanie. "With sunflowers. They make me think of you!"

Just then, a small sparkling cloud appeared in the sky.

Willow frowned. "I hope it's not another windstorm!"

The sound of wind chimes filled the air, and Willow's mood went from *gray* to *yay!* as a tiny golden box floated down from the cloud . . . and right into her hands.

"A new badge!" Jeanie gasped.

Willow opened the box to find a scroll and a badge embroidered with a paper plane in golden thread. The scroll said:

In recognition of your latest work, we are pleased to award you the Fly-Away badge.
Congratulations!

Sincerely,
The World
Genie Association

Willow beamed. She was one step closer to becoming a Master Genie. Jeanie put an arm around her. It had been another magical adventure for the two best friends!

LOOK FOR MORE

# Jeanie & Genie

BOOKS AT YOUR FAVORITE STORE!